PHONY FRIENDS, BESTIES AGAIN

The Continuing Adventures of Emo and Chickie

Gregg F. Relyea and Joshua N. Weiss

Illustrated by Vikrant Singh

Kayla Weiss, Contributor

About the Authors

Gregg F. Relyea, Esq.

Gregg F. Relyea is a professor of law at the University of San Diego School of Law, California Western School of Law, and University of California, San Diego (UCSD), teaching negotiation, mediation, and alternative dispute resolution. He has been called upon by numerous governmental agencies, courts, and corporations to provide mediation training, including the United States Department of Justice, the United States State Department, the San Diego Superior Court, the Hong Kong International Arbitration Centre, the Supreme Court of India, the High Courts of Delhi, India, Bangalore, India, Chennai, India, and Ahmedabad, India. He has also conducted mediation training for various non-governmental agencies in the United States and around the world. Mr. Relyea was a guest of honor at the 2018 International ADR Summit in Delhi, India, where he moderated panels, provided training, and served as a valedictory speaker to close the conference. He is a frequent guest lecturer for specialized programs, including the Osher Lifelong Learning Institute (University of California, San Diego), the San Diego Association of Realtors, and in-house training programs at law firms and other organizations. Mr. Relyea is an experienced workplace investigator, working with corporations to understand claims of discrimination and harassment, and wrongful termination.

Gregg F. Relyea is a full-time mediator, professional negotiator, international trainer and lawyer. He helps people resolve legal, governmental, complex commercial, and interpersonal disputes. As a professor of law, he teaches key principles and advanced skills of constructive conflict resolution. As a mediator, Mr. Relyea applies these principles and skills on a regular basis with everyday people, litigants, and organizations.

Joshua N. Weiss, Ph.D.

Dr. Joshua Weiss is the co-founder of the Global Negotiation Initiative at Harvard University and a Senior Fellow at the Harvard Negotiation Project. He is also the Director and creator of the Master of Science degree in Leadership and Negotiation at Baypath University. He received his Ph.D. from the Institute of Conflict Analysis and Resolution at George Mason University in 2002. Dr. Weiss speaks and publishes on leadership, negotiation, mediation, and approaches to resolving conflicts.

Both authors have published numerous articles about conflict resolution in professional journals and they have produced instructional videos in various formats, including YouTube.com, blogs, podcasts, and other websites.

Phony Friends, Besties Again

Copyright © 2019 by Gregg F. Relyea and Joshua N. Weiss

**Resolution
Press**

ISBN-13: 978-0-9998344-8-0

Praise for Phony Friends, Besties Again

Bill Richardson, Former Governor of New Mexico and Former US Ambassador to the United Nations

"The lessons here are invaluable for kids and adults alike. We can all learn from the language and techniques in this book to communicate effectively and to solve problems. Kids who learn these skills at an early age will become the world's future negotiators and diplomats."

Sheila Heen, Lecturer on Law, Harvard Law School, and Co-author of the bestselling book, *Difficult Conversations—How to Discuss What Matters Most*

"Phony Friends offers a wonderful catalyst for talking with our kids about that confusing crossroads of social media, popularity and friendship. Follow Emo and Chickie as they navigate the joys of capturing juicy footage, the temptations of posting and instant celebrity, and the rough road of understanding the impact it has on each other—and on themselves. This new episode is sure to spark important conversations for kids and adults alike."

Jim Melamed, CEO of mediate.com

"Emo and Chickie have a falling out, yet manage to somehow work things out using a variety of 'modern forest' communication devices that young and old will relate to and be humored by. My favorite is using 'Forestgram' for communication. Emo and Chickie getting back together is the result of clarifying emotions, intentions and communications, all woven together with both 'online' and 'face-to-face' communications. Emo and Chickie's effective communication is a model for young and old alike also beyond the forest."

Dr. Clare Fowler, Managing Editor at Mediate.com, ADR professor at University of Oregon School of Law

"The Relyea and Weiss team have done it again. They have managed to slip fundamental truths into an easy-to-read format. My kids love reading these books because of the warm graphics and the funny characters, and they don't even realize they are learning dispute resolution concepts that they will draw on for the rest of their lives."

Kenneth Cloke, Mediator, Teacher, Dispute Resolution Systems Design, Commentator and Author of *The Dance of Opposites: Explorations in Mediation, Dialogue and Conflict Resolution Systems Design*

"Many of the conflicts faced by children result from misunderstandings between friends. This new book by Gregg Relyea and Joshua Weiss explores the higher order skills that are required in order to make and keep friends. But instead of preaching or lecturing, which often feels punitive, these skills are presented as a story, which encourages empathy and deep learning. We need entire libraries of books like these."

Forrest "Woody" Mosten, Mediator, Collaborative Lawyer, Teacher and Author of *Mediation Career Guide—A Strategic Approach to Building a Successful Mediation Practice*

"Research has shown that children who have conflict resolution training not only improve their problem-solving skills but also better stand up to bullying. By introducing these skills to young children through lovable animals and grabbing illustrations, Gregg Relyea and Joshua Weiss offer life lessons, helpful perspectives, and conversational tools that children can immediately use with their friends and families--and refine over time as they grow. The hidden treasure in Phony Friends, Besties Again *is that adult readers of the book get a Master Class for their own lives and work. As a professional mediator for over 40 years who read this book to my 5-year-old grandson, I can attest to its immediate and, no doubt, lasting impact on both of us."*

Jeffrey Krivis, Mediator, Past President International Academy of Mediators, Mediation Trainer and Author of *Improvisational Negotiation—A Mediator's Stories of Conflict About Love, Money, Anger, and the Strategies That Resolved Them*

"Teaching children how to think, through storytelling and art, is the code that unlocks a good moral character. This book provides the key to that door."

Emily Weinstein, Ed.D., Social Media Researcher, Harvard Graduate School of Education

*"*Phony Friends, Besties Again *provides a timely entry point for important conversations about friendship in the age of social media. Is it okay to post something funny even if it might embarrass a friend? How can you respond if a friend shares something online that hurts or embarrasses you? Characters Emo and Chickie thoughtfully navigate age-old social challenges related to "real" and "phony" friends in a world complicated by Owlphones and apps like Forestgram. They model crucial social skills as they engage in self-reflection, cooling off, clear communication about tricky emotions, active listening, apologizing, and forgiveness. Few issues are more relevant for today's kids than social media's impact on emotions and friendships, and* Phony Friends, Besties Again *offers a relatable story that is purposefully woven with positive messages."*

Carla Marcucci, Family Law Advocate and Past President of the Italian Association of Collaborative Professionals

"In the series, The Adventures of Emo and Chickie, *first through the book,* Trouble at the Watering Hole, *next through the book,* Bullied No More! *and now with* Phony Friends, Besties Again, *Gregg Relyea and Joshua Weiss provide powerful tools to enable children to learn about conflict resolution in a fun and effective way. Gregg and Joshua's genius idea is introducing children to interest-based negotiation right from the start, as with reading, writing and math, instead of waiting until adulthood, when it becomes more and more difficult to make the paradigm shift away from positional bargaining."*

Dr. Debra Dupree, President/Founder, Relationships at Work, Inc. and Author of *Leading Consciously Now*

"Conflict is inevitable anytime two people come together with differing beliefs, expectations, attitudes, concerns and hopes…not to mention fears, values and needs. The "what" of conflict often is an issue, yet it is "how" conflict is managed that makes all the difference. Teaching children effective ways of navigating through conflict builds character, integrity and a personal sense of self that will last a lifetime. Phony Friends, Besties Again, from authors Gregg Relyea and Joshua Weiss, will be a powerful engine for positive social change in years to come."

Sriram Panchu, President, Association of India Mediators, Author of *Settle for More, Mediation Practice and Law* and *The Commercial Mediation Monograph*

"One little story and what a huge impact. The child learns that conflict can be resolved by opening up and talking, understanding others, and making relationships matter. And best of all, that the two children can do this themselves. There is no better antidote to the spread of conflict than to implant this lesson at an early age. Other lessons of wisdom are gently embedded. Listening to an inner voice. Thinking about the impact of actions. Choosing friends carefully. And being mindful about the hasty use of social media. This is a superb example of a children's book being of great value - and not just to children."

Emo and Chickie's Conflict Resolution Books

Trouble at the Watering Hole
Trouble at the Watering Hole Coloring Book
Bullied No More!
Phony Friends, Besties Again

Available in paperback and eBook
through all major booksellers.

Acknowledgments

The authors would like to acknowledge the inspiration for the book by Mr. Niranjan Bhatt, a lawyer from Ahmedabad, India, who inquired years ago about the availability of books about conflict resolution skills for children. His question sparked the idea for a series of illustrated storybooks, the first children's books to present concrete core skills for resolving conflicts through storytelling: *Trouble at the Watering Hole, Bullied No More!* and *Phony Friends, Besties Again.*

We are thankful to our students who educated us about their daily, hourly, and, at times, minute-to-minute use of social media as well as the types of conflicts that frequently arise. They reported that most social media conflicts resulted in some form of social disconnection, including unfriending, blocking, or deleting accounts, leading to an ever-deepening reservoir of unresolved social media conflict.

In addition to outstanding editorial assistance, Brian Moreland provided invaluable expertise in the production of the book in a variety of formats.

Catherine Loverde contributed a unique and insightful perspective about children's experiences and how they relate to the world. In addition, she provided valuable editorial assistance in making the book readable and relatable to young children.

With unsurpassed attention to detail, John Ross helped to put the finishing touches on the manuscript. His command of proper, idiomatic, and colloquial grammar shaped a book that is comfortable for young children to read and absorb.

Kayla Weiss helped with many early drafts of the manuscript, brainstorming storyline ideas, and offering useful insights. She also contributed valuable research on social media conflict.

We also wish to acknowledge the encouragement and fresh perspectives about collaborative dispute resolution from Carla Marcucci, an Italian family lawyer, founding member and Past President of the Italian Association of Collaborative Professionals (AIADC, *Associazione Italiana Professionisti Collaborativi*), and a leading advocate for the constructive resolution of family disputes.

To all the young people preparing for life in a socially interactive and technology-filled world. And, to all those parents and teachers helping kids navigate through everyday conflicts, both small and large. It's not random luck, magic, or natural ability only that successfully resolves conflict—it's listening, opening up about one's needs, learning what's important to others, and finding solutions that benefit everyone.

—Gregg Relyea

To all those families and friends who have lost meaningful relationships to destructive conflicts. Remember, conflicts are started by people and can be resolved by those same people with hard work and creative thinking.

—Joshua N. Weiss

On the last day of winter vacation, the sun was shining and the weather was mild for January. The animals gathered around the frozen watering hole. Some were slipping and sliding along the ice. Others played with their Owlphones, taking pictures, selfies, and videos.

Best friends, Emo and Chickie, joined in the fun. Hanging out with friends was cool, but what everyone really liked was seeing themselves on their phones and sharing pictures with each other. It made them feel famous--like they were on TV. Emo leaned back against a big rock. "Chickie, we've been friends since we were little. Have you ever enjoyed hanging around this much?"

Chickie agreed, "No way! I'm glad we get to have some fun on the last day before school!"

On the first day of classes, the animal kids scurried to Forestville Elementary in bad weather. Strong winds and heavy snow on the ground made walking tricky.

All bundled up in thick coats and hats, they were careful to step around the icy patches along the sidewalk. Some students were enjoying the last few minutes before school --again taking pictures, selfies, and videos.

In front of the school, Chickie waited for his best friend. Like most days, Emo was running late.

As Emo waved to Chickie, he did not notice the icy patch on the sidewalk under his feet.

Just for fun, Chickie grabbed his Owlphone and started recording a video of Emo.

Suddenly, Emo slipped on the ice. His feet flew out from under him, legs shooting into the air. He let out a loud "Yelp!" and landed hard on his stubby tail.

Emo lay flat on his back. Everything hurt. He was afraid to get up. He didn't even want to look at the other animals who saw him wipe out.

How embarrassing! Emo thought as he picked himself up.

Even though he was Emo's best friend, Chickie could not help but laugh out loud with all the other animals.

Emo looked like he was about to cry as he stuffed his books into his backpack.

Chickie forced himself to stop laughing and stopped recording.

He went over to his friend and asked, "Are you OK?" while trying hard not to laugh.

Still in pain, Emo struggled to answer, "I guess so, but that fall really hurt."

"I bet it did," said Chickie.

"And, I'm feeling really embarrassed," Emo added, looking around at all the kids laughing at him.

After Chickie helped Emo gather his things, the two friends went into the school together.

At lunch, a fox and a little deer sitting at the popular kids' table were talking about how funny Emo's wipeout was.

Sitting nearby, Chickie overheard the conversation. He flew over to the popular kids and said, "I know, I got the whole thing on video."

Max, a fox who was leader of the cool kids, replied, "No way, can I see?"

For a second, Chickie hesitated. His inner voice told him not to show anyone the video, but it didn't seem like a big deal. As he let the popular kids watch the video, they howled with laughter. Chickie got swept up in the moment and laughed as well.

Max said, "You *have* to post this video to Forestgram! It is too hilarious not to!"

Chickie knew it might embarrass Emo, but he got carried away. *Why not post the video?* Chickie thought to himself. *It's not a big thing. It's all in good fun anyway.* Besides, Chickie really enjoyed the feeling of hanging out with the popular kids ... finally!

Chickie opened his Forestgram app and, with a simple *Click!*, he posted the video, even though he wasn't thinking much about the impact of his actions.

Emo came into the lunchroom looking for Chickie. He was sitting with some popular kids Emo didn't know. *Hmm . . .* Emo thought, *I've never seen Chickie sitting with those kids before.*

Emo sat at the table across from his bestie. "Hey, Chickie."

Chickie looked up. "Oh, hey, buddy." Chickie then turned his attention back to his new friends.

The other kids at the table kept laughing and snickering. Emo didn't know what they thought was so funny, so he just started eating his lunch.

Shortly after Emo sat down, the other kids got up to leave.

"Hey, Chickie," Max said, "want to walk to class with us?"

"Sure!" Chickie joined the group, barely saying goodbye to Emo.

Emo ate his lunch alone. He noticed that Chickie had dropped him to be with the cool kids.

After school, Emo loaded his backpack and started walking outside. A group of kids were gathered around an Owlphone, laughing.

As Emo walked by, he heard his voice coming from the phone, so he stopped and looked over their shoulders. They were watching a video of him falling . . . on Forestgram!

Emo turned red with embarrassment. He just wanted to get out of there.

Once outside the school building, Emo wondered who posted the video, so he looked on his phone. The Forestgram page read: Posted by Chickie at 11:45 a.m.

That can't be right, Emo thought. *Why would Chickie do that to me?*

Emo walked home with his head down. He just wanted to disappear. As he kept playing that video in his mind, his sadness turned to anger.

He asked himself, *Why would my best friend embarrass me? He's never done anything like that before.*

Along with his anger, Emo felt hurt and confused.

Needing an explanation, Emo took out his Owlphone and texted Chickie, "Hey, did you record my wipeout and post it on Forestgram?"

Minutes later, Emo got a *bing* on his phone. Chickie replied, "Yes, I did. Hope you don't mind, but it was really funny and the other kids thought it would be cool to share the video."

Now, Emo was REALLY mad. He wrote back, "Of course, I mind! A lot! The whole school is laughing at me. Take that post down right away!"

Chickie wrote back, "OK, OK. Relax. It's no big thing. I'll take it down later."

Relax? What was Chickie saying? All Emo could think to text back was, "I will relax when you take the video down. Do it NOW!"

"Whatever!" was Chickie's only reply.

Emo was so angry he turned off his phone so he couldn't see any new messages from Chickie.

Meanwhile, Chickie was angry too, so he typed a mean message making fun of Emo for everyone to see. He started to push the "Send" button, but he just couldn't do it. Chickie felt he hadn't done anything wrong, but he knew that, if he didn't work things out with Emo, he could lose Emo's friendship for good.

The next morning, Emo was getting ready to leave for school.

Chickie texted him, "Hey buddy, want to walk to school together?"

Emo only replied, "No!"

When Emo got to school, he saw Chickie talking with the popular kids. They were laughing and joking. Max, the fox, pointed at Emo--clearly making fun of him.

What is happening? wondered Emo. He was really hurt.

He sent Chickie a text, "We need to talk."

Hours later, in the afternoon, Chickie finally answered Emo's text, "OK, let's talk tomorrow."

A cold and dreary day at school came and went.

After finding Chickie, Emo started talking, "Chickie, why did you post that video? It was so embarrassing for me and now the whole school has seen it."

Chickie looked at Emo, "Oh c'mon, where's your sense of humor? It wasn't that big of a deal. Besides, I never meant to make you feel bad."

Emo replied, "Whether it's a big deal or not isn't for you to decide. I'm the one who looked like a fool. And you think it's funny!"

Chickie was surprised by Emo's reaction. "OK, but I think you're making a much bigger deal about this than it really is. You need to chill."

Emo stared at Chickie, who was making excuses for what he had done. Emo was so angry he didn't know what to say. "This is not working, Chickie. We need to stop talking. It's just making me madder. We will have to try talking again later." Emo stomped off.

Chickie called to him a few times, but finally gave up.

This is all Emo's problem, Chickie thought. He flew back to school to find his new friends.

As Chickie joined his new friends, he was confused. On the one hand, Emo was his best friend and he seemed really mad.

Chickie's new friends were more laid back and funny. As their conversation continued, Chickie thought less about Emo and more about the fun he was having. It felt so good to be one of the cool kids. All it took was posting a silly video of Emo falling down and Chickie became liked by everybody.

But, deep down, Chickie's feelings were all mixed up. He had lots of questions. *Would he ever be friends with Emo again? Was it worth it to make new friends by embarrassing Emo? Even though he didn't mean to hurt Emo, was it wrong to post the video?*

Chickie pushed away these thoughts. He was simply having too much fun being part of the cool crowd. While it felt wrong to turn his back on his best friend, Chickie told himself he just didn't care and that Emo was making a big deal out of nothing.

Emo moped around the house all weekend. His parents asked him what was wrong. All he could think to say was he didn't feel good. He didn't want to tell them he had trouble with Chickie. It was just too embarrassing.

Finally, on Sunday evening, his mother said, "Emo, you're playing with your food. What's wrong, dear?"

Emo couldn't keep his feelings bottled up inside any longer. He told his mom and dad everything: slipping on the sidewalk at school, the kids laughing at him, Chickie posting the video on Forestgram, and everyone at school seeing the video. After he finally opened up and talked about it with his parents, Emo felt better, but he was still mad at Chickie.

"Have you tried working something out with Chickie?" his mother asked.

"Yes, but he didn't seem to understand." Emo sighed.

His mother suggested, "Maybe you could have another talk with him. Chickie might need some time to think about things."

Emo's father added, "It might help if Chickie looked at the situation from your point of view." He left Emo with a question, "How do you think you could get him to do that?"

Emo answered, "I'll try to think of something."

As Monday came around, Emo left his house early to avoid crossing paths with Chickie on the way to school. Emo was not ready to talk again yet.

He was surprised to see Chickie fly down from his perch to be next to him. At first, Emo wanted to ignore him, but he was still so upset, he couldn't help himself.

"What has gotten into to you?" Emo yelled.

Chickie was startled. "What do you mean? I didn't do anything! You're the one who is so sensitive!"

Emo stopped. He took another deep breath. "We need to sit down and talk this out. We have some time before school. We've been friends for a long time."

"OK." Chickie sat next to Emo on a log near a pine tree.

Just as they started to talk, Chickie's phone buzzed. He stopped listening to Emo. All of Chickie's attention was on reading somebody's new text on his phone. It was Max, inviting Chickie to play with him and his friends.

Emo blew up. "Can't we just put down our phones for one second and talk to each other?"

Not really wanting to, Chickie turned off his phone. Emo did the same.

Emo began, "Can you see why I am upset and hurt? When I fell the other day it was painful, but also really embarrassing. It was bad enough that all the kids around me saw it happen, but then you posted that video and now the entire school is laughing at me. Let me ask you this: if I had posted an embarrassing video of you, wouldn't you be mad?"

Wow, I never thought of it that way, Chickie admitted to himself.

After thinking about it, Chickie replied, "I guess I can see why that would make you mad. I wasn't trying to hurt you. It was funny and the other kids thought so too."

Emo sighed. "I'm sure it was funny as long as it didn't happen to you. And then, to make things worse, you started hanging around with all the popular kids and left me out."

"I did not," Chickie explained, "the other kids just didn't invite you . . . that was their decision."

"But you went along with it. Did you ever ask them if I could come too?" asked Emo.

"No," Chickie replied. "Listen, Emo, it's **OK** for us to have other friends. We don't need to spend all our time together."

"I know that," Emo said, "but making new friends is *not* the issue. It was the way you shared the video on Forestgram for everyone to see. What you did really hurt my feelings."

"I never thought about that," said Chickie. "You're absolutely right, Emo. It was wrong for me to post the video. And I should have asked my new friends to include you. I'll ask them when we get to school. Maybe we can all hang out together!"

Emo smiled. "Thanks, Chickie. I appreciate it. I really didn't like being mad at you, but I guess sometimes this happens, even between really good friends."

"I'm the one who should apologize," Chickie said. "What I did was not nice and I gave in to what my new friends asked me to do. It felt good to be part of the cool crowd. I'm really sorry, Emo."

The two friends did a fist bump and stood up to walk to school together.

Later that day, Chickie went over to his new friends and spoke to their leader, "Max, I was wondering if Emo could hang out with us at lunch today. He's really a great guy and has been my best friend for a long time."

Max laughed. "We're not hanging out with that big clumsy clown. If you want to be friends with him, you need to make a choice --us or him."

Max's response totally surprised Chickie. Not knowing what to say, he smiled and flew away with a quick, "OK, see you later."

As Chickie flew down the hall, he realized his new cool friends were, well, not so cool after all. *How could he have not seen this before? How could Max treat Emo so badly?*

All of a sudden, Chickie felt really sad.

Seeing Emo's big furry ears sticking up in the crowded hallway, Chickie flew up to talk to him.

"Emo," Chickie said, "I'm so sorry, but my new friends, well, they're not really my friends at all. They liked me when I was not being nice to you. When I asked if you could join the group, they were mean about it. If that's how they feel, then I don't want to be friends with them. I'm deleting that video post right now. Can you ever forgive me?"

Emo broke into a smile. "I think so, buddy. But, can I trust you again?"

"100%!" Chickie chirped.

"Good to have you back, Chickie! I'm glad you understand." Chickie jumped on Emo's arm as Emo invited him to hang out. "How about we go to the watering hole today after school?"

"You got it, buddy, but I have to do one thing first," Chickie said.

As they were leaving school, Chickie spotted Max among the group of popular kids. Chickie pulled him aside. "Max, I can't be friends with you if you won't also accept Emo. He's my best friend and if you don't want to include him, then I guess you'll have to leave me out too."

Max shot back, "WHATEVER!" as he walked back to the group, laughing and pointing at Chickie.

Even though that hurt, Chickie knew he had done the right thing.

As Emo and Chickie walked to the watering hole, the sun began to shine brightly. Even though there were patches of snow on the ground, the warm sun felt good on their faces.

They sat down next to a nice big rock near the watering hole. Everything was in its place again. The animals were all there, enjoying the sunshine, laughing, and playing with their phones.

As they sat together, both Emo and Chickie felt good again. Yes, a conflict had come up between them. But, in the end, they worked it out by opening up about their feelings, listening to each other, and learning what was important to each of them.

Emo and Chickie, at long last, were besties again.

WHEN CONFLICT COMES UP, EMO AND CHICKIE TEACH US TO:

ASK QUESTIONS

LISTEN CAREFULLY

IMAGINE HOW THEY'RE FEELING AND SAY SO

SHARE WHAT'S IMPORTANT TO YOU

LEARN WHAT'S IMPORTANT TO OTHERS

THINK OF IDEAS THAT BENEFIT EVERYONE

<u>Questions you can ask to learn about
a person's concerns and needs:</u>

1. Help me understand what's important to you?

2. What are your main concerns?

3. What matters most to you?

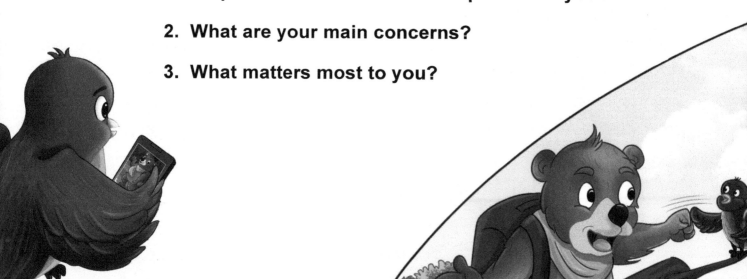

For more information about the skills that can be used
to resolve social media conflict, read the article:

Educating the Next Generation in Resolving Social Media Disputes
by Gregg F. Relyea

https://www.mediate.com/articles/relyea-educating-next-generation.cfm

Printed in the USA
CPSIA information can be obtained
at www.ICGtesting.com
CBHW080041051223
2374CB00023B/753